Bob
HELPFUL
THE ROBOT

To Eleanor Grace

B.W.

EGMONT

We bring stories to life

First published in Great Britain 2006
by Egmont UK Ltd
239 Kensington High Street, London W8 6SA
Text and illustrations copyright © Bob Wilson 2006
Bob Wilson has asserted his moral rights
ISBN 978 1 4052 1594 7
ISBN 1 4052 1594 1
10 9 8 7 6 5 4 3 2 1
A CIP catalogue record for this title is available from the British Library.
Printed in Singapore.

Contents

Red Bananas

THE MYSTERIOUS NEIGHBOUR

The man who sold Tom's mum and dad their new house didn't tell them about the man who lived next door.

But after they moved in everybody did.

'He's odd,' said the postman. 'He gets some really peculiar parcels.'

'He's weird,' said the window cleaner. 'His kitchen is full of strange contraptions.'

'He's a bit loopy,' said the girl in the hardware store. 'He once bought thirteen bicycle pumps.'

'Why?' asked Tom.

She didn't know.

Tom found out more from the lady in the paper shop. She said the man's name was Professor Plum. She said, 'He's a raving loony.'

'What does he do in there?' asked Tom's dad.

She didn't know.

What she did know was that sometimes strange noises came from the shed.

Such as ... **BING BANG BONG** and ... **CLUNK CLICK WHIRRR.**

And once there had been a tremendous explosion that had blown the roof right off.

When Tom's mum was told about this she got quite upset.

'Oh, I wouldn't worry,' said Dad. 'I'm sure she was exaggerating.'

But then, a little later, he said,

On the other hand, it might explain why our garden is like it is.

9

Mum warned Tom, 'Don't you ever go near that shed.'

Don't even think about it.

But Tom did think about it. And the more he thought about it the more curious he became. He wondered what Professor Plum might be doing in the shed. Perhaps he was a mad scientist doing dangerous experiments?

With this potion I shall conquer the world!

Maybe he was an alien from another world, disguised as a human, and was building a space ship so he could get back to his own planet.

One small step for a Martian. A giant leap for a garden shed.

A few weeks later he found out.

A LOAD OF RUBBISH!

It was a beautiful morning.

The first day of spring.

Dad was inspired.

> Today I shall tidy the garden.

'I'll give you a hand,' said Mum.

'Me too,' said Tom.

> I'll give you two hands.

He'd been looking forward to playing in the garden all winter.

Tom used to live in an apartment at the top of a tower block. He had lots of friends but nowhere to play.

I said no footballs in the living room.

That was the reason his mum and dad decided to move.

'You'll have a lovely garden to play in at the new house,' said Mum.

With a lawn, and big trees to climb.

'Will I be able to have a swing?' said Tom.

'Yes,' said Dad.

'And a slide to slide down?'

'Of course,' said Dad.

'And will you make me a play-house with a look-out post and a mast and a rope-ladder and flags and a sail?'

Dad looked a bit doubtful. 'You want me to make you a play-house that looks like a pirate ship?'

'Yes please!'

'OK. I will,' said Dad. 'If I get time.'

'Dad's got to tidy the garden up first,' explained Mum.

It's in a bit of a mess.

She wasn't kidding.

The house had been empty for a long time.
People seemed to have
been using the
garden as
a dump.

But today, at last, they were going to sort it out.

'Brilliant,' said Tom. Soon he was going to have a proper garden to play in with a swing and a slide and maybe even a play-house. 'Brilliant,' he said again.

Mum and Dad worked in the
garden all morning.

It was hard going. It wasn't long
before Mum's back had given way.

I can't
straighten up.

And Dad had lost
all his enthusiasm.

I'm too old for
this lark.

By lunch time they'd both had enough of it.

It's a much bigger job than I thought.

We don't have to do it all now.

But Tom was still keen.

Come on in now, Tom. Your lunch is going cold.

I'm just doing this.

'Will you be putting up my swing today?'
asked Tom, after lunch.

'Probably not today,' replied Dad. 'Maybe
tomorrow.' And he went to have a lie down.

Tom turned to Mum. 'Will Dad make me
a slide tomorrow too, d'you think?'

'Probably not tomorrow,' replied Mum.
'Maybe next week.'

Tom let out a long sigh. He didn't even
bother to ask about his play-house. It would
probably be next century before Dad found
time to make him a pirate ship play-house.

He went outside, sat down among the rubbish, and sulked. He was fed up and lonely. He'd got no new friends and his garden was a dump.

Just then he heard a noise. It was coming from next door. It sounded like somebody was coming out of the shed.

Was it the mad Professor?

He climbed on to a box. He peeked over the fence.

And he got a surprise.

It was a girl.

The girl looked up at Tom, and smiled. 'Hello,'
she said. 'My name's Daisy.'

'I'm not allowed,' said Tom, sadly.

'Why not?'

He told Daisy what people had said about
Professor Plum.

'That's not true!' said Daisy. 'Grandad isn't dangerous. He's kind and cuddly – and he's not a nut-case. He's an inventor.'

'Professor Plum is your grandad? And an inventor?' Tom was really interested now. 'What's he inventing?'

'Come and see,' said Daisy. 'You'll be amazed.'

So he did.

And he was.

Wow! It's a robot!

SAY HELLO TO HELEN

'This is my bicycle-pump-automated, aurally-activated, command-motivated robot,' said Professor Plum, proudly.

'She's called "Helpful Helen",' said Daisy, 'because of what she does.'

'What does she do?' asked Tom.

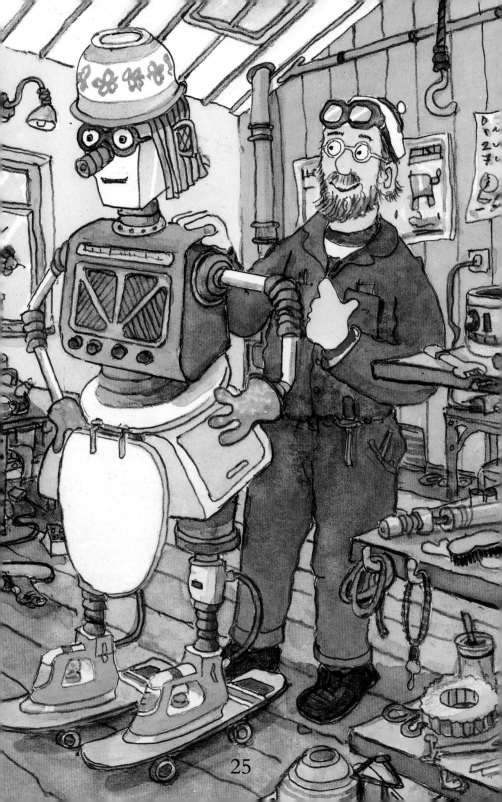

'I'll show you what she can do,' said Professor Plum.

Watch this.

The Professor turned a knob on the robot's chest radio and its eyes lit up. Then, pointing to a bucket on the floor, he said, 'Helen ... See ... That ... Bucket? Pick ... It ... Up ... And ... Put ... It ... On ... The ... Shelf.'

And Helpful Helen said,

I ... HEAR ... I ... DO ... WHAT ... YOU ... TELL ... ME ... TO.

'Wow! That's amazing!' exclaimed Tom.

Your grandad's really clever.

Tom wanted to know what else the robot could do.

'Anything,' she replied. 'You just have to tell her to do something – and she does it.'

'Actually it's not quite that simple,' said Professor Plum. 'You have to speak slowly, be very careful what you say, and only tell her to do one thing at a time.'

Otherwise she gets mixed up.

28

'Helen always does exactly what I tell her to do,' said Daisy. 'It's easy.'

This remark gave Tom a brilliant idea. Turning to Daisy's grandad, he said, 'Professor Plum?'

Would Helen do some jobs for me?

'Of course,' replied Professor Plum. 'What sort of jobs did you have in mind?'

'Clearing up a messy garden sort of jobs,' replied Tom.

HELEN COMES TO HELP

Mum and Dad were back working in the garden. Mum was painting the fence. Dad was at the end of the garden fixing the gate.

'Look who's here,' said Tom.

Mum was taken by surprise.

'It's a robot called Helpful Helen,' said Tom. 'She's come to help you with your jobs.'

When Dad heard this he came rushing over. 'Jobs? Did you say it does jobs? What sort of jobs?'

What will it do?

'Anything you tell her to do,' said Professor Plum.

'But you have to speak slowly,' said Tom.

'And be careful what you say,' said Daisy.

'Can it use a hammer?' said Dad.

'CAN . . . HIT . . . USE . . . HAM-MER,' said Helen.

'Brilliant,' said Dad.

Can it paint?

CAN . . . HIT . . . PAINT

'Yes,' said Professor Plum. 'But be warned, you must only tell her to do one thing at a time, otherwise she'll get mixed up.'

This warning came a little too late. Helen was already getting mixed up.

HIT . . . PAINT-CAN. USE . . . HAMMER.

But Dad didn't notice – and he didn't heed Professor Plum's warning either. He was too excited. 'If it can hammer and paint that's great,' he exclaimed. 'But before it does that, it can go ahead and tidy up this garden.'

'I . . . HEAR . . . I . . . DO . . . WHAT . . . YOU . . . TELL . . . ME . . . TO,' said Helen.

CAN . . . GO . . . ON . . . HEAD.
HAMMER . . . UP . . . GARDEN.

'Not so fast, Dad,' said Tom. 'You're getting her mixed up!'

But Dad took no notice. He bounded up to Helen and said, 'See this garden?'

'SEA . . . IS . . . GARDEN,' said Helen.

'It needs tidying up.'

'TIDE . . . IS . . . UP,' said Helen.

'I want it looking ship shape.'

SHIP . . . SHAPE?

That's what I said – SHIP SHAPE.

'I want all these pipes and oil cans on the rubbish tip.'

'ALL . . . PIPES . . . CANNONS,' said Helen.

But save those boards. I might make use of them for decking.

'BOARDS . . . FOR . . . DECK,' said Helen.

'Get that, robot?' said Dad.

'GET . . . WHAT . . . ROW-BOAT?'

Helen was clearly confused but Dad wasn't listening.

Right. Next job.

FOR
ALE

This ladder's not wanted – or this rope.

'WANT . . . KNOT . . . ROPE-LADDER.'

This For Sale sign's to go. Those sacks want moving and I want a post putting up for the clothes line.

'POST FOR SALE,' said Helen.

And I could do with you rigging up some trellis for these roses to climb up.

'RIGGING . . . TO . . . CLIMB . . . UP.'

Get that, robot?

GET . . . WHAT . . . ROW-BOAT?

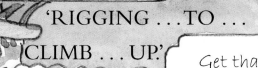

By the time Dad had finished his list of jobs Helen was utterly confused.

GARDEN . . . IS . . . SEA . . . TIDE . . . IS . . . UP.
MAKE . . . DECK . . . CANNON . . . POST . . . SAIL
. . . ROPE-LADDER . . . RIGGING . . . ROW-BOAT . . .
AND . . . CLIMB . . . ABOARD.

She doesn't know what to do.

But then she remembered what Dad had said at the start, and exclaimed, 'GOT . . . IT!'

YOU . . . WANT . . . EVERYTHING. . . SHIP . . . SHAPE.

'That's it,' said Dad. 'You've got it exactly.'
And he and Mum went happily back into the
house to have a cup of tea.

Meanwhile, Tom, Daisy, and Professor Plum
watched as Helen set to work. They were a
little worried. It didn't look as if she was
clearing up the garden.

'I think she might be
building something,' said
Professor Plum.

'Like what?' asked Daisy.

'I've absolutely no idea,' replied the
Professor. 'We'll just have to wait and see.'

After a while everything became clear – to Tom at least – and he exclaimed, 'I've got it! I think I know what she's building, and if I'm right . . .'

Twenty minutes later, Professor Plum popped his head round the living room door.

'Why? What's happened?' said Mum.

'Has that robot of yours done what I told it to do?' said Dad.

'Oh, yes,' replied Professor Plum.

43

WELL, STRIPE ME PINK!

Everyone came to see Tom's pirate ship play-house.

They thought it was wonderful.

They told Tom's dad he'd made a really good job of building it.

'It wasn't Dad who built it,' said Tom.

It was Daisy's grandad.

They all stared at Professor Plum.

'Well I never,' said the postman.

'Well, who would have thought it?' said the lady from the paper shop.

'Me,' said the girl from the hardware store.
'I would have thought it.'

I told Tom how clever you were.

So did I.

Me too.

And me.

Tom didn't say anything.

BOOM!

Professor Plum was a modest man. He said, 'Actually I wasn't the one who built Tom's playhouse. It was Helpful Helen.'

'Helpful Helen?' they all said. 'Who's Helpful Helen?'

Helen was next door, painting Daisy's bicycle. She heard them say her name. Her head popped over the fence. Everyone was taken by surprise.

I . . . HEAR . . . I . . . DO . . . HOW . . . ME . . . HELP . . . YOU?

'Well, I'll be blowed!' cried the postman.

'Well, I'll eat my hat!' exclaimed the lady from the paper shop.

'Well, stripe me pink!' shouted the window cleaner.

'No. You mustn't shout things like that!' cried Tom.

But his warning came a little too late.

'I . . . HEAR . . . I DO . . . WHAT . . . YOU . . . TELL . . . ME TO,' said Helen.

IN . . . A . . . WINK . . . I . . . STRIPE . . . YOU . . . PINK!